HONEST TULIO

JOHN HIMMELMAN

BridgeWater Books

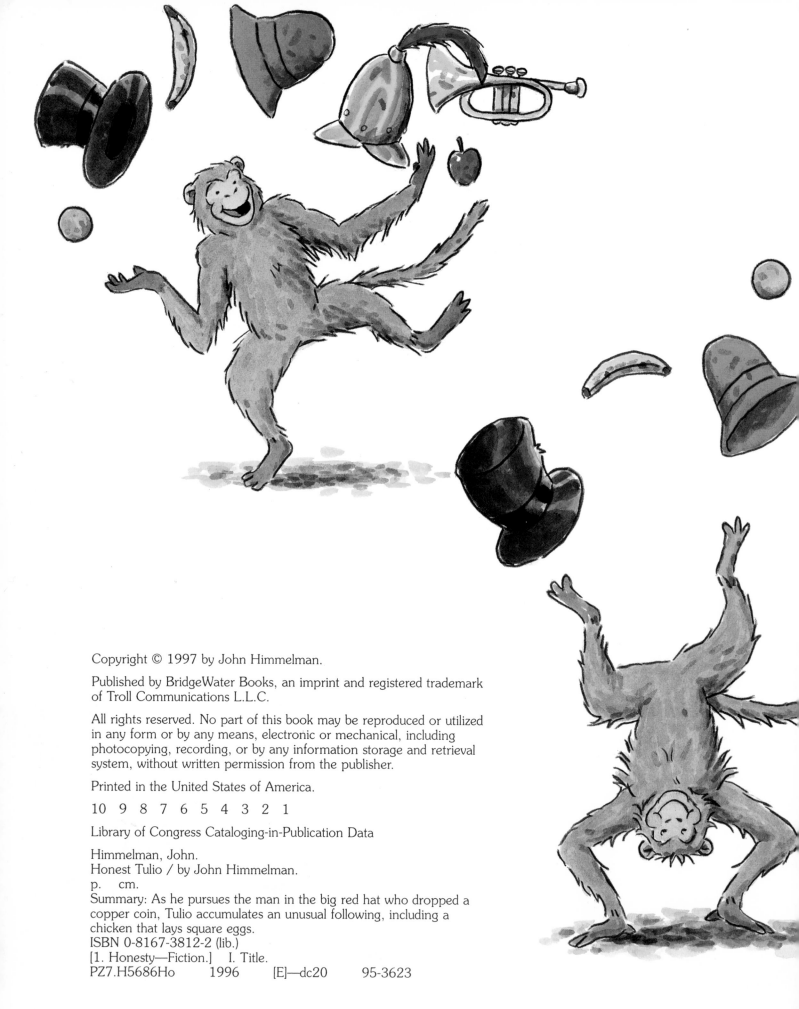

Published by BridgeWater Books, an imprint and registered trademark of Troll Communications L.L.C.

Printed in the United States of America.

10   9   8   7   6   5   4   3   2   1

Library of Congress Cataloging-in-Publication Data

Himmelman, John.
Honest Tulio / by John Himmelman.
p.   cm.
Summary: As he pursues the man in the big red hat who dropped a copper coin, Tulio accumulates an unusual following, including a chicken that lays square eggs.
ISBN 0-8167-3812-2 (lib.)
[1. Honesty—Fiction.]   I. Title.
PZ7.H5686Ho   1996   [E]—dc20   95-3623

For my wife, Betsy, my most important collaborator.

JH

Tulio lived in a large wooden crate by a busy marketplace. He had no mother or father, but he had many friends who looked out for him.

Everyone liked Tulio.

"That Tulio is as honest as the sun is bright," they said.

To earn his meals, Tulio did chores for the market vendors. Someday I will have my own stand in the market, he thought. That was his dream.

One day, as Tulio was delivering a basket of apples, he saw a man in a big red hat drop a copper coin. Tulio picked up the coin and tried to catch the man.

"Sir, sir, you dropped your coin!" he shouted. But it was very busy at the marketplace, and the man got lost in the crowd. Tulio worked his way through the people and saw the man in the big red hat ride off on a horse.

A passing farmer gave Tulio a ride in the back of his hay wagon. The wagon moved too slowly to catch the man in the big red hat. But Tulio would not give up.

"This is as far as I go," said the farmer. "Good luck catching that man. You are as honest as a rock is hard." He gave Tulio a lamb's-wool coat to keep him warm.

Tulio hurried up the dirt road. A traveling circus was heading the other way. A man stood on the side, yelling at an elephant. "If you won't do tricks, you can't stay with the circus!" he shouted.

"You shouldn't yell at elephants like that," said Tulio.

"If you love elephants so much, you take her," said the man. "She comes with this juggling monkey, too. He juggles everything he can get his hands on, and it drives everyone crazy!"

Tulio rode off on the elephant with the juggling monkey. Way in the distance, he saw the man in the big red hat, getting on a boat. "Hurry!" said Tulio to the elephant, but he was too late. The boat had left.

Suddenly, Tulio heard a scream. "My royal poodle has fallen into the water!" It was the queen herself. All of her royal guards were trying to fish the poodle out of the water.

"Do something! Do something!" cried the queen.

Tulio rode up on the elephant with the juggling monkey. The elephant reached into the water and pulled out the royal poodle.

"You saved her," said the queen. "Please accept my gift. It is a royal hat in the shape of the royal poodle, and it comes with royal guards to protect it."

Tulio felt a little silly in the hat, but he didn't want to hurt her feelings. After all, she *was* the queen.

"Thank you," he said. "Do you know where I can get a boat? I need to return a copper coin that was dropped by a man in a big red hat."

"Young man, you are as honest as a poodle is curly," said the queen.

Soon Tulio, wearing the royal poodle hat guarded by the royal guards, sitting on the elephant with the juggling monkey, was sailing on a swift ship to catch the man in the big red hat.

He almost caught up with the man in the big red hat on the other side of the river. But once again, the man got lost in the crowd. A parade was marching down the street. Tulio passed through the parade. When he came out of the crowd, he still heard music. The marching band thought he was part of the parade, and it was following *him.*

Tulio saw the man in the big red hat climb into a wagon and race toward the hills. Tulio, wearing the royal poodle hat guarded by the royal guards, followed by the marching band, sitting on the elephant with the juggling monkey, raced after him.

He traveled day and night, but the man in the big red hat stayed far ahead of him. Suddenly the ground began to shake. Tulio held on tight as the sun disappeared behind dark shadows.

He looked up to see five thirty-foot-tall giants dancing to the music of the marching band.

"We love the pretty music," they rumbled as they spun and whirled around him.

Way in the distance, Tulio saw the man in the big red hat. Sitting on the elephant with the juggling monkey, Tulio sped off in his royal poodle hat guarded by the royal guards, surrounded by five giants dancing to the marching band.

Finally, Tulio caught up with the man in the big red hat. But it was not the man he was looking for! This man was one of seventeen other men in big red hats. The seventeen men carried seventeen bags of corn. In the seventeen bags of corn were seventeen holes. Flocks of hungry chickens surrounded them, eating the corn that spilled from the holes.

"Where are you going?" asked Tulio.

"We are searching for a seamstress to stitch up the seventeen holes in our seventeen bags of corn," they said.

"I am looking for a different man in a big red hat. He lost a copper coin, and I must return it to him."

"You are as honest as corn is yellow," they said. "We will join you. We men in big red hats stick together."

Just then, one of the chickens landed on the elephant. It laid an egg.

"Oh, my! This egg is square! This is the strangest thing I've ever seen!" said Tulio, as he sat on the elephant with the juggling monkey, wearing his royal poodle hat guarded by the royal guards, surrounded by five dancing giants dancing to the marching band, followed by seventeen men in big red hats who were carrying seventeen bags with seventeen holes leaking corn eaten by flocks of hungry chickens.

As he headed toward town, word spread quickly of Tulio and his search. People waved and hollered as he rode by.

"He is as honest as a pie is round!" they shouted.

"He is as honest as a moose is big!" they cheered.

"He is as honest as a cheese is smelly!" they trumpeted.

Tulio smiled and waved back, but he didn't understand why everyone was so excited. I am only doing what any honest person would do, he thought.

Tulio looked down at the people. There, in the middle of the crowd, was the man in the big red hat. Tulio took off his royal poodle hat and climbed down from the elephant. He raced over to the man in the big red hat.

"Sir, sir, I've found you at last. You dropped a copper coin," he said. He reached into his pocket to pull out the coin, but his pocket was empty. The coin had fallen through a hole. Tulio felt very bad.

"That's okay," said the man. "It was worth it to see the beautiful show you have brought us!"

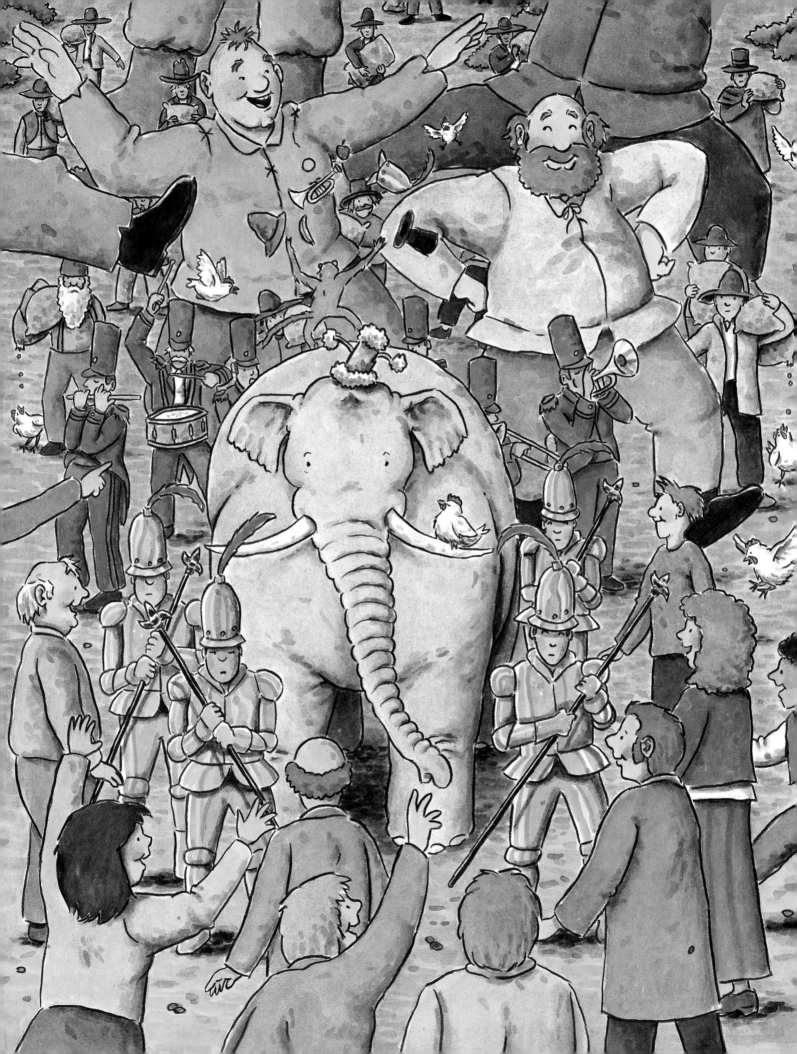

But Tulio wasn't satisfied. He looked back at the crowd around the royal poodle hat guarded by the royal guards, surrounded by five dancing giants dancing to the marching band, with seventeen men in big red hats who were carrying seventeen bags with seventeen holes leaking corn eaten by flocks of hungry chickens, next to the elephant with the juggling monkey and the chicken that laid square eggs. Then he had an idea.

"I can't give you back your copper coin, but I can leave you with something else instead," Tulio said.

The man with the big red hat was very happy.

Tulio was very happy. He headed home, keeping only two of the things he had found on his journey.

The lamb's-wool coat from the very kind farmer. And the chicken that laid square eggs.

Tulio's dream finally came true. He opened his own market stand and did very well selling the only square eggs in the world.

"That Tulio," his friends all said. "He is as honest as his eggs are square!"